Lobster Boat

Brenda Z. Guiberson

illustrated by Megan Lloyd

Henry Holt and Company ✦ New York

To Laura Godwin, for her wisdom, support,
and kindness in the creative process
—B. Z. G.

For Jack and Jean, who expanded my horizons,
and showed me how to put a lobster to sleep
—M. L.

The artist wishes to thank Dana and Mike,
the crew of the *Shady Lady*.

Text copyright © 1993 by Brenda Z. Guiberson
Illustrations copyright © 1993 by Megan Lloyd
All rights reserved, including the right to reproduce
this book or portions thereof in any form.
First edition
Published by Henry Holt and Company, Inc.,
115 West 18th Street, New York, New York 10011.
Published simultaneously in Canada by Fitzhenry & Whiteside Ltd.,
91 Granton Drive, Richmond Hill, Ontario L4B 2N5.

Library of Congress Cataloging-in-Publication Data
Guiberson, Brenda Z.
Lobster boat / written by Brenda Z. Guiberson; illustrated by Megan Lloyd.
Summary: Tommy spends the day on a lobster boat helping Uncle Russ
tend the traps, set bait, pull up the traps, and sell their catch.
ISBN 0-8050-1756-9
[1. Lobster fisheries—Fiction. 2. Sea stories.]
I. Lloyd, Megan, ill. II. Title.
PZ7.G93833Lo 1993
[E]—dc20   92-4055

Printed in the United States of America
on acid-free paper. ∞

1 3 5 7 9 10 8 6 4 2

The early morning is crisp and cool and dark. Fog touches the tiny town on the coast and blurs the warm yellow lights in the houses and the red-orange leaves on the trees. Two dark figures glide over the water in a dory. A woman in big waterproof boots clomps into the bait shop. *Aaa-oooooo.* The blast of a foghorn comes from a boat in the harbor.

Crreeeak! Behind a small gray house, the door of a fish shack opens. Tommy walks out with two yellow slickers and big waterproof pants that are crumpled and stained. His uncle Russ carries a bucket of fish heads and trimmings. "Will we really go out today?" says Tommy. "Look at all this fog." Russ picks up a thermos of cocoa and starts down the cobbled path to the beach. "The sun will burn it off," he says. "C'mon." *Aaa-oooooo.* The mournful tones of a foghorn reach Tommy and the brown dog as they follow Russ through the mist.

At the beach, the tide is very low. Russ unties the rowboat and drags it down to the water. When Tommy climbs in, the bottom of the boat scritch-scratches across the rocky ocean bed. "We'll need more bait," says Russ as he rows them away from the shore.

Tommy points straight ahead through the fog. "There she is," he says. "There's our lobster boat, the *Nellie Jean*."

When everything on the lobster boat is stowed away, Russ pulls on his waterproof pants and warms up the diesel engine. Then he drives across the harbor to a long weathered dock.

Old Sam and Ginny come out and help Tommy load two more buckets of fish bait. "The storm brewing out there should go south," says old Sam. "That's the report," replies Russ. *"We're* going fishing." Old Sam rubs his fingers across the brim of his hat. "Well, so am I," he says. Tommy coils the thick ropes that hold the boat. "Go get 'em," says Ginny as she and old Sam push the lobster boat away from the dock.

The *Nellie Jean* moves through the harbor. *Scree! Scree!* Sea gulls smell the bait in the buckets and fly in close. "Scram, you rascals," says Tommy. "Too early for your breakfast." He covers the buckets with a yellow rain slicker. Russ pushes the throttle forward for extra speed and follows the ghostly shape of a big boat with towering masts and long, dangling ropes. *Aaa-oooooo. Ooo-aaaaaa.* The foghorns sound. The lobster boat sways and totters in the deep waves churned up by the huge boat. The smell of diesel mingles with the everlasting odor of fish and sea.

Flicker-blink. The faint glow from the lighthouse reaches out through the fog to the *Nellie Jean*. Russ uses it to steer safely past jagged rocks that stick out above the sea. The boat jumps and jitters over the foamy waves that crash around the rocks. Carefully, very carefully, Tommy pours two cups of hot, steaming cocoa.

Soon the fog burns off and the bright blue-green of the ocean glistens in the sunlight. *Scree! Scree!* More sea gulls follow the *Nellie Jean* with noisy chatter. Russ lines up the boat with a distant white cliff to keep her headed in the right direction. "Uncle Russ!" Tommy shouts loud into the wind. "Are we going to move the traps out into deeper water?" Russ shakes his head. "Not yet. Most of the lobsters seem to be moving across the gravel bottom, right by the traps we put in last week."

Russ squints across the bright ocean as he guides the boat. Soon they pass a group of painted buoys that are tied to lobster traps under the sea. The red-and-white ones belong to the Jensen brothers. Old Sam paints his buoys with orange stripes. Tommy grins when he sees the ones painted yellow on top and red on the bottom. Everyone knows that these belong to the lobster crew of the *Nellie Jean*. Throttle back, out of gear. Russ nudges the boat alongside their closest buoy.

Tommy reaches out to hook the rope coming from the buoy. Russ slings it around the automatic winch and turns on the switch. *Wirrrrr.* The winch grinds and groans, slowly pulling up a lobster trap that has been sitting on gravel bottom one hundred feet below the sea. The dripping rope brings water, seaweed, and a tiny crab into the boat. *Scree! Scree!* Sea gulls come so close that Tommy feels a wing flap against his shoulder.

When the trap reaches the surface of the water, Tommy pulls it to the railing of the *Nellie Jean.* The trap is covered with furry sea growth and is slippery in his hands. *Click, click.* Reddish-black lobster claws reach out through the wires and a pair of lobster antennas twitch in the salty sea air. "Looks like we got ourselves a big one," says Russ.

Tommy opens the back door of the trap and carefully grabs the lobster from behind. *Click, click* go the crusher and ripper claws. *Click! Clack-click!*

"Look at this female," says Tommy. "Loaded with eggs." Russ shows Tommy where to make a notch in her tail. "No one will keep her now," he says, "even when she isn't carrying eggs."

Tommy puts the lobster back into the sea,
where she will protect her eggs for months
and months until they are ready
to hatch.

Tommy reaches in for another lobster. "Too small," says Russ. *Click, click. Sssplash.* Another lobster goes back into the sea. Tommy takes out the last one. "Better measure it," says Russ. Tommy fits a brass gauge between the eye sockets and the end of the body shell. The lobster is three-and-a-half inches long and big enough to keep. Russ slips a thick rubber band over each claw. The lobster squirms and wiggles, but the claws do not open. This lobster goes into a bucket of seawater.

Tommy takes the old bait from the trap and throws it into the air. *Scree! Scree! Screeee!* Finally the noisy sea gulls get their breakfast. They swoop down and catch some of the soggy fish before it hits the water. Tommy uses the baiting iron to load new fish frames onto the bait string in the trap. "I'll check the depth finder," says Russ. "I don't want to drift away from that gravel bottom where all the lobsters seem to be traveling."

Russ watches the gauge and pulls hard on the steering wheel to make a sharp turn. When he nods his head, Tommy pushes the freshly baited trap overboard.

The lobstermen move on from trap to trap. They work quickly and check twenty, then fifty, then more than a hundred traps. The buckets fill up with lobsters and sea gulls fill up with old bait. They find two traps that are damaged and replace them with new ones.

As the warm, sunny day turns blustery, Russ keeps a watchful eye on the darkening sky to the south.

On the way to another trap, Russ gets a call on the radio. "New weather report," says old Sam, who is fishing nearby. "That squall has changed its mind and is headed right this way." Tommy looks over to see the dark clouds moving in fast. Both of them pull on yellow slickers and long oilcloth hats. Throttle full ahead, they start back to the harbor.

A strong wind comes in to lash at the water and
rattle through the wheelhouse. Waves swell up white
and foamy and Russ leans his whole body against
the steering wheel to help keep it steady.

Howling, crashing, the full storm rages around the *Nellie
Jean*. Seawater slaps the bow and pounds on the window.
Tommy slips and slides across the deck as he ties down the
traps and buckets. The pelting rain turns his face bright red.
The boat groans and moans and rattles everywhere.

Flicker-blink. The double flash of the lighthouse reaches
them through the drenching rain. As they near the harbor, the
wind shifts and turns up the coastline. Gradually the sea loses
its choppy whiteness and Tommy is able to stand up straight.
He gets out a brush and pail and begins to clean up the lobster
boat. Sea urchins, small crabs, and piles of dangling seaweed go
back into the sea.

The *Nellie Jean* looks clean and tidy as Russ steers her through a crowd of boats coming in from the storm. He pulls the boat up to the lobster pound. Ginny is there to weigh the lobsters. "The good news is that you caught more than old Sam," she says. "The bad news is that the catch is high everywhere and the price is down."

Ginny decides to keep these lobsters in a lobster pound, a
fenced-in cove where she will feed them for several months. In
winter, when lobsters are hard to catch, Ginny can sell them for
a higher price. She pays Russ and Tommy, and they get gas for
the *Nellie Jean* and tie her up to her moorage in the harbor.
Then they row back to the gray house by the beach.

Russ cooks something to eat. The smell of broiling steak mingles with that of the salty air. Tommy sits on the back porch and weaves a new funnel-shaped door for an old trap. They listen to the latest weather report when they sit down to eat. *Sunny and cool.*

"Do you think the storm damaged many of our traps?" asks Tommy. "Maybe the shallow ones near the rocky ledge," says Russ. "The rest are deeper and should be safe."

It is dark again in the tiny town on the coast. Chains clank, boats creak and sigh in the wind, bright leaves rustle under the trees, small waves *sa-woosh, sa-wiish* onto the beach. Only the flash of the lighthouse remains to keep watch over the harbor. *Flicker-blink…Flicker-blink.* Soon it will be dawn and another day of lobstering for the crew of the *Nellie Jean*.

Lobster, Lobster, Where Is the Lobster?

Lobstermen and -women must know many things if they want to catch lobsters. They need to know about the ocean, weather, boats, fishing gear, and the rules of the people who fish in the same area. But in order to have the most success, what they need to know best of all is the lobster itself.

In the summer, lobsters go through a molting period, when they shed their outer shells. During this time they are weak and soft and not interested in eating. They prefer to hide in the mud and rocks of warm, shallow water. This is not the best time of year to go looking for lobsters. After the molt, the lobsters are in a growing period and are very hungry. Many young lobsters will reach the minimum legal size and lobstermen will be able to keep them if they are caught. Late summer and fall are the times when the lobster catch is greatest.

As the weather cools and the shallow water gets cold, lobsters migrate across the ocean floor to deep, warmer water. Using depth sounders and lots of experience, the lobstermen try to find out which way the lobsters are moving and place their traps nearby. In the winter, lobsters hibernate under rocks or burrow into mud and do not eat much. Some lobstermen continue to put out traps, but they do not check them as often and the catch is much smaller.

In the spring, the lobsters move back into shallow water, but by this season most legal-size lobsters have already been caught.

With record numbers of lobsters caught in recent years, how can we be sure that the supply of lobsters will remain sufficient? The fishing system of the lobstermen helps to preserve their industry. Female lobsters that are caught are returned to the sea to produce eggs for future generations. Only lobsters of a legal minimum and maximum size are kept. Groups of lobstermen limit the number of competing traps in their area by making it difficult for new lobstermen to get started. These measures have helped to maintain a reasonably steady supply of lobsters in the sea.